Smell My lephant

Last Saturday, after he had made his bed, Fletcher brewed a pot of tea to share with Elephant. The tea was just right: medium brown with a thin swirl of golden honey. But something was out of the ordinary.

Elephant drank his tea in one gulp, like usual, and then watched and waited for Fletcher as quietly and as calmly as ever. But Elephant smelled different, Fletcher noticed.

Everyone knows that stuffed elephants smell like all the places they've ever been:
    the pantry,
        the sandbox,
            the laundry basket,
                the dog's bed.
But last Saturday, Fletcher didn't know what Elephant smelled like. So he decided to ask for help.

Fletcher found his mom first. "Excuse me, Mom?"
he asked. **"Smell my elephant."**

"Whoa," she said. "He smells like dirty socks.
I think it's time for a bath."

Fletcher sighed and said, **"No. Not dirty socks."**

Next, Fletcher found his dad. "Excuse me, Dad?"
he asked. **"Smell my elephant."**

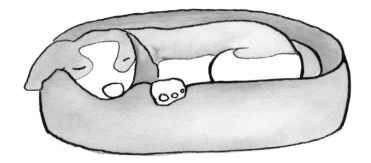

"What in the world? He smells like popcorn," Fletcher's dad said. "Was your elephant sneaking snacks again?"

Fletcher grinned and said, **"No. Not popcorn."**

Big sisters always know, Fletcher thought. He found Iris outside. **"Smell Elephant,"** he said.

"Okay. But first, he needs a crown," Iris said.

Fletcher and Elephant watched and waited patiently. The crown was just right. Fletcher thought it made Elephant look magnificent, and Elephant seemed to like it too.

"He smells like clover blossoms to me," Iris said.

Fletcher laughed and said, **"No. Not clover blossoms."**

Just then, Fletcher heard a familiar voice.

"Fletcher! Hey, Fletcher!" his friend Henry called to him. "Rocketship 1D1 is leaving in

ten...

nine...

eight...

seven..."

But Fletcher wasn't prepared for a moon mission. His goggles
and space map were inside, under his bed. Besides, he needed
to know what Elephant smelled like before lunch, because
after lunch Elephant always—no matter what—smelled like
strawberry jam.

"Maybe later," Fletcher said.

"Okay. I can wait," Henry said. "Or we can play robots if you want."

"I'm smelling Elephant right now," Fletcher said. "He smells different."

"Can I smell?" Henry asked.

Elephant didn't seem to mind as Henry held him close, sniffed one ear and then the other, and, after a few seconds, said, "Honey, beetle wings, I think, and maybe rubber boots. He smells like you."

Fletcher pulled Elephant back into his arms. "Me?" he asked and sniffed Elephant again. "Maybe that is me! And I smell Iris." **SNIFF**. "I think I smell Mom and Dad, too."

Fletcher finally knew just what Elephant smelled like.

"Elephant smells like hugs!"

Fletcher smiled, hugged
Elephant, and went inside to
fetch his goggles and find out
if it was almost time for lunch.

Sleeping Bear Press™
2395 South Huron Parkway, Suite 200
Ann Arbor, MI 48104
www.sleepingbearpress.com

Printed and bound in the United States.

10 9 8 7 6 5 4 3 2 1

Library of Congress Cataloging-in-Publication Data

Names: DeBord, Tina Ballon, 1980- author. | DeBord, Kim Jackson, 1977-illustrator.
Title: Smell my elephant / written by Tina Ballon DeBord ; illustrated by Kim Jackson DeBord.
Description: Ann Arbor, MI : Sleeping Bear Press, [2017] | Summary: After asking family members
    to identify his toy elephant's strange smell, a young boy discovers the loving answer.
Identifiers: LCCN 2016030978 | ISBN 9781585369928
Subjects: | CYAC: Toys--Fiction. | Smell--Fiction.
Classification: LCC PZ7.1.D399 Sm 2017 | DDC [E]--dc23
LC record available at https://lccn.loc.gov/2016030978